D1403556

VORTEX

VORTEX

VANESSA ACTON

MINNEAPOLIS

Darby Creek
A division of Lerner Publishing Group, Inc.
241 First Avenue North
Minneapolis, MN 55401 USA

For reading levels and more information, look up this title at www.lernerbooks.com.

Front cover: © iStockphoto.com/cosmin4000; © iStockphoto.com/Marina Mariya (swirl).

Images in this book used with the permission of: © iStockphoto.com/cosmin4000 (tornado); © iStockphoto.com/Marina Mariya (swirl).

Main body text set in Janson Text LT Std 12/17.5.
Typeface provided by Adobe Systems.

Library of Congress Cataloging-in-Publication Data

Names: Acton, Vanessa.
Title: Vortex / Vanessa Acton.
Description: Minneapolis : Darby Creek, [2017] | Series: Day of disaster | Summary: "What do you do when you and your family are in the middle of a road trip when a tornado hits?" Provided by publisher.
Identifiers: LCCN 2016014145 (print) | LCCN 2016028379 (ebook) | ISBN 9781512427738 (lb : alk. paper) | ISBN 9781512430950 (pb : alk. paper) | ISBN 9781512427806 (eb pdf)
Subjects: | CYAC: Tornadoes—Fiction. | Survival—Fiction.
Classification: LCC PZ7.1.A228 Vo 2017 (print) | LCC PZ7.1.A228 (ebook) | DDC [Fic]—dc23

LC record available at https://lccn.loc.gov/2016014145

Manufactured in the United States of America
1-41498-23359-7/1/2016

Cupp
PZ
7
,A1838
Vo
2017

For Mrs. Wassermann, a champion among school librarians, who can face down the eye of any storm

The day of the disaster, Blair O'Neill actually thought her weekend was improving.

She and her brothers had survived their mom's wedding. Now all they had to do was get home to Michigan.

They'd left on schedule, exactly at eight. One hour down, twelve to go. Blair's older brother, David, was driving, as usual. Her younger brother, Logan, sat in the back—earbuds in, eyes closed. Blair was in the front passenger seat. She'd offered to drive part of the way, since she had her permit now, but no luck. "You can drive us around once you have your license," David had told her. "For now you'll be my copilot." Really, the GPS was his copilot. Blair was just moral support.

"I'm so glad to be out of there," David said as the car's clock blinked to *9:02 a.m.*

"I noticed," said Blair. Her older brother had been visibly tense ever since they arrived in Hatchville, South Dakota. He'd hardly said anything to their mom. Gritted his teeth through the overdue introduction to Theo, their mom's fiancé—now her husband. Barely smiled in the wedding photos. Didn't dance or mingle at the reception. For a guy who'd just turned twenty-one, he'd acted a lot like a cranky uncle—more so than usual.

"I almost wish we hadn't come at all," he mumbled now, his eyes on the road. "It's not like Mom would've missed us."

Blair tried not to flinch. She was used to hearing this from David. For a long time she'd felt the same way. But it had been six years since their mom left. Weren't they old enough to know better now? "Come on, Dave, that's not true." Sure, their mom was flaky, but that wasn't the same as not caring. And she'd wanted her kids at this wedding, for sure. She'd even offered to pay for them to fly out—an offer David had refused.

David made a dismissive noise in his throat. "Now that she's got Theo, it's like she's forgotten Dad even exists. And we're right on the edge of falling off her radar along with him. Mom only ever thinks about what *she* wants to do, what'll make *her* happy—not about what she leaves behind."

From the backseat, Logan said to David, "Well, Theo's definitely way cooler than Dad. So there's that."

Blair whipped around to glare at her twelve-year-old brother. His eyes were still closed. Blair knew David wouldn't have said so much if he'd known Logan was listening. Then again, Logan wasn't an innocent six-year-old anymore. It had been a long time since he'd needed David to tell him bedtime stories or arrange his food in smiley faces. A long time since Logan had burst into tears at any mention of their absent mom, or thrown a tantrum whenever their dad drove off on yet another business trip. He was old enough to hear what his siblings really thought—and to be obnoxious about it. "Don't you have some death metal to concentrate on?" she snapped.

"It's not death metal. It's *doom* metal. Blackened doom. And Theo is, like, at least twenty percent cooler than Dad."

"Logan, do me a favor. Shut up until you're past puberty."

Logan responded with a gesture she ignored.

"Take it easy," said David, out of habit.

Blair faced forward again and stared at the road. Not an inspiring view. Just a two-lane highway, empty except for David's car. Surrounded by basically nothing: bare fields on either side, cloud-clogged sky above, the occasional tree or fence or distant farmhouse. Blair hadn't realized that South Dakota was so *flat*. It was ridiculous. "If this is what it looks like here in May, people must gouge their eyes out in the wintertime."

David managed a weak laugh. "Guess you won't be moving in with Mom and Theo?"

"Never." She looked over at him, but he kept his eyes on the road. The smile on his face wasn't real. It was the same smile he'd used all weekend, at all the awkward moments—the smile of a guy who expected to be let down.

Blair didn't know what to do about it. Except promise not to move to South Dakota.

For the past six years, she and David had been a team, taking care of things while Dad was at work—which was most of the time. Their dad had dealt with the divorce by burying himself so far into his job that he was barely home, which meant that Blair and David had to pick up the slack. Doing the laundry, learning to cook, looking out for Logan. Looking after their dad, too, in a lot of ways. When had David gotten bitter about it? Blair wasn't sure.

Better question: When had she *stopped* being bitter? Little by little, without really noticing it, she'd forgiven her mom for leaving and her dad for never being around. David hadn't.

That was his choice, of course. Blair couldn't tell him how to feel. But she wished she'd been able to enjoy her mom's wedding. She liked Theo—and she liked her mom, honestly. If David hadn't been so obviously miserable, Blair might've actually had a good time.

She wished David would let her drive. That would give her something else to think about.

"I don't like the look of that sky," David said.

He had a point. It had been cloudy all morning but now the clouds looked heavier—darker. They hovered so low to the ground that they looked close enough to reach up and touch.

Blair pulled out her phone. "Want me to check the forecast?"

"Yeah. Maybe put the radio on too. See if we can find a local weather station."

Blair had already pulled up her weather app. "Hold on—my phone still thinks I'm in Michigan."

She plugged in *Hatchville, South Dakota*. They were already an hour east of her mom's home, but it was the only decent-sized town in the area. Blair wasn't even sure anything else would show up on a map.

The phone's screen flashed with warning icons. "Whoa, there's a tornado watch—for, like, the entire state."

"Did you say tornado watch?" asked Logan. Apparently he'd paused the blackened doom.

"Just a watch, not a warning," David said quickly.

"What's the difference?"

"A watch just means conditions are right for a tornado to form," Blair told him. "A warning means a tornado's actually been spotted." Tornadoes weren't common where the O'Neills lived. But as an outdoor lifeguard last summer, Blair had gotten a crash course in weather safety. And she'd heard her mom's stories. Five years of living in Tornado Alley had made her mom an expert.

"Cool," said Logan. "Wake me if there's a warning. I'm gonna take a nap."

David's hands had tightened on the wheel. "Turn on the radio, Blair."

Blair hit the AM button on the dashboard. She didn't even have to scan channels. A staticky voice was in the middle of a weather report.

. . . and as far east as Mathison County. If you're in those areas we advise you to stay indoors.

Once again, folks, we have a major storm system moving north. There is a tornado watch in effect for much of north central Nebraska and southern South Dakota . . .

The announcer ran through the list of affected counties again. Blair checked the GPS screen. The O'Neills were in Tate County, just east of Mathison County—right on the edge of the storm system. Off to Blair's right, in the depths of the thick clouds, lightning flashed.

"Sounds like the storm system's southwest of us," said David. He sounded calm—but he always sounded calm. Even when he was angry, he kept his voice flat and distant. The flatter and more distant, the more emotion he was holding in. "And we're heading away from it."

"Sort of," said Blair. "We're going straight east. It's moving north and east."

"We should be fine if we keep going." Still, Blair saw the speedometer's needle inch upward.

The voice on the radio talked through the static . . . *Line of supercells forming across south central South Dakota . . .*

Blair still remembered the statistics she'd looked up when her mom first moved to South Dakota. Only about ten percent of storms are supercells—thunderstorms with rotating air currents. And only about twenty percent of supercells produce tornadoes. Plus, most tornadoes happen in the late afternoon and evening, not in the morning. All of which meant that the O'Neills had good odds of *not* seeing any twisters today.

Blair's phone buzzed. Her mom had texted her. *Weather looks bad—moving east. Are you guys near White River yet?*

Not yet, Blair texted back. *But I think we're ahead of the storm. It's not even raining here.*

Good. Just be careful.

You too. Tornadoes were business as usual for Blair's mom by now. She and Theo had a hardcore storm shelter. They used it so often that Theo jokingly called it their summer home. No need for them to climb into their bathtub, like their neighbors who didn't have basements or shelters. Hatchville had never actually been hit by a twister, though. Just plenty of watches, warnings, and near misses.

Another flash of lightning, high up in the dense mass of clouds off to the right. Blair squinted.

Those clouds . . . they looked as if they were slowly rotating.

"Um, Dave?" Blair tried to keep her voice neutral. For years, she'd copied him in a lot of ways, but she'd never quite mastered his *keeping-it-together* tone. "I think we should pull off the highway at the next town. We don't want to get caught in this."

David looked doubtful. "It'd probably be best if we just keep going. We should be out of range pretty soon."

Blair bit her lip. Was she imagining it, or was the churning motion becoming more distinct? *Only twenty percent of supercells produce tornadoes.*

But she kept her eyes glued to the sky. Five minutes . . . ten minutes . . . until, in the center of the slow-turning cloud mass, she saw something new.

A narrow finger of gray-black vapor, twisting downward.

"Dave, that's a funnel." Blair's voice spiked with fear. "That's an actual funnel." Instinctively, she grabbed the handle of the passenger door, just for something to hold on to.

The spiraling upside-down cone was growing by the second—reaching toward the ground.

"Okay, okay, don't panic."

Fair enough. That was step one of surviving any crisis. Good start. But what next?

Fragments of warnings and tips rattled around in Blair's head: things she'd learned from her lifeguard training, from talking to her mom, from her own Internet research. *Do not take shelter in a vehicle. Do not take shelter under an overpass. Do not try to outrun a tornado. Get inside. Stay inside.*

"We need to get off the road, Dave!" They had no cover out here. This land couldn't have been any flatter if someone had bulldozed it.

And the car would offer no protection against a twister's massive wind power.

"Okay, see where the nearest town is."

Blair glanced at the car's GPS. It showed her nothing but the dot of her brother's car and the east-west line of the road. She pulled up a map on her phone. "Twenty miles away. It's called Aura."

"Oh, yeah—I saw a sign for it, a ways back. We need to stop for gas soon anyway. We can make a stop in Aura. And if the sky still looks bad at that point, we'll wait there until this blows over. But that funnel might not even touch down—and even if it does, it might not come our way. We need to stay calm, Blair."

Easy for you to say, she almost snapped. Then she saw his hands: knuckles white on the wheel. He was as freaked out as she was. But he was trying to focus, trying to plan their next move. Just like he'd done every day for the past six years.

Blair breathed out. "Okay. I'll look up what's in Aura—see what businesses are closest to the highway. There's probably a convenience store or someplace like that—someplace we can duck into until we're sure the coast is clear."

David nodded approvingly. "Good idea."

Blair enlarged the map on her phone screen, found a gas station located right off the highway, and plugged its address into the car GPS. By the time she looked back out the window, the funnel was hovering much closer to the ground. Wisps of brown dust and dirt swirled up from the earth, rising to meet the twister.

"Logan," she said over her shoulder. Her voice wavered, but only a little. "You might want to wake up now."

"Wha . . . why?"

"Look out the window. To your right."

A moment later, Logan yelled, "*Whoa!* I gotta get a video of this!" Blair looked back at him. He was holding up his phone, pointing it at the tornado.

The funnel had made contact with the ground now. The mini-cloud of dirt and dust at its base was growing. "Dave, it's touched down," Blair told her older brother, whose eyes were still glued to the road in front of them. "It's the real thing." And she wasn't sure yet, but . . .

"Wow, that is *close*," said Logan.

Now she was sure.

Blair's chest tightened. "It's coming our way!"

2

"Guys—" yelped Logan. "It's actually moving toward us! It's coming right at us!"

"We noticed!" Blair snapped.

"It's moving *fast*!"

"Go, Dave!" Blair stopped trying to keep her voice level. "Go, go, go!"

"I'm going!"

Blair felt the car speed up, but it didn't seem to make a difference. The tornado was bearing down on them. With each second, it filled more and more of the view from Blair's window.

"We're almost to Aura," David said.

Blair heard—and felt—the wind pick up. Rain started battering the car. David switched on the windshield wipers and kept a tight grip on the wheel. Blair could tell he was struggling to keep the car from swerving.

Even the voice on the radio sounded urgent now. Blair heard blips of information through the static.

. . . reports of multiple touchdowns in Mathison and Tate counties . . . take shelter . . . very dangerous situation . . . tornadoes on the ground . . .

Logan had stopped filming. He seemed to be looking up something on his phone. "We need to take shelter in a ditch!" he shouted.

So *now* he was taking this seriously? Blair twisted around to look at him. "Do you see a ditch? Tell me where you see a ditch!"

"We have to find low ground!"

"There is no low ground! This whole area is completely flat! There's nowhere to take shelter!"

"We can't outrun that thing!" Logan yelled. "It's right on top of us!"

"I know!" she yelled back.

The realization hit her in the gut, then

traveled up to her throat, burning in her mouth like vomit. *We're not going to make it to Aura.*

The rain was coming down in a thick, slanted curtain. The road in front of them became a blur. Blair felt the car losing traction, sliding on the slick concrete. David slowed down, clearly afraid of spinning out if he drove too fast.

Then, a huge tree branch slammed into the car. A spider-web of cracks shot across the windshield.

Before Blair could even scream, the branch was gone—blown away from the car as fast as it had been blown toward it.

Blair curled up in her seat, knees tucked against her chest, hands over her face. "Dave, stop! Just stop! You can't—"

Every side window in the car shattered at once.

No time to react. Glass showered over Blair. She shrieked, more from shock than pain, but the howling wind drowned out the sound she made. She felt her ears pop.

David was shouting at the top of his lungs—loudly enough that Blair easily heard him through the vacuum in her ears.

"Are you guys okay? *Are you guys okay?*"

The car had stopped. The windshield wipers—one warped, one mostly gone—swept back and forth with a high-pitched scraping noise. The rain was still coming down—coming through the broken windows now, stinging as it hit Blair's skin. Shards of glass dusted her whole body. She saw a few small scratches on her arms but didn't feel them. "I'm okay," she croaked. "Logan?"

She turned to look at the backseat. Logan stared at her, stunned. "I think my phone is gone."

"Forget your phone, idiot! Are you hurt?"

"Uh, no? No, I guess not. There it goes." He pointed to Blair's left. Blair turned back around. Through the splintered front window, she saw the tornado moving away from them. Its outer edge must've just grazed them as it crossed the road.

"Man, that was close." Blair looked over at David—and almost screamed again. "Dave! Your arm!"

Her older brother stared blankly at the blood running down his right arm. "Piece of glass must've hit me," he said in a dull, distant voice.

"You think?!" *Stop that*, Blair told herself firmly. *You're panicking. Focus. Remember your first aid training.* "Let me see it."

"Let me just turn on the emergency lights—"

"David! Let me see your arm!"

The blood wasn't spurting—good. That meant the glass hadn't hit an artery. But the cut went deep, and the bleeding was steady. Must be a vein. "We need to put pressure on that. Where's the first aid kit?"

"Uh, somewhere in the trunk, I think."

"Okay, hold your arm above your head." She grabbed it and lifted it for him, then took his other hand and clamped it on top of the wound. "Press down as hard as you can." She reached across him and hit the button to pop the trunk. "I'll be right back."

Blair didn't stop to take a breath before she opened the car door. That was a mistake. The force of the wind and rain hit her full force now. The tornado might be gone, but the rest of the supercell thunderstorm still hovered overhead.

Blair braced herself against the car as she staggered around to the back. The emergency lights blinked feebly onto the rain-soaked road behind her.

She couldn't remember the last time she'd seen another car. Were the O'Neills all alone out here? Was everyone else in South Dakota hiding underground?

The hail started just as she raised the trunk's lid.

The first chunk hit her in the shoulder. Then three more, *bam-bam-bam* on her head and back. Then a shower. It felt like being pelted with golf balls. Blair instinctively held a hand over her head to shield herself, but that was pointless. She needed both hands to sort through the mess in the trunk.

So much junk in there. Their overnight

bags. Her bridesmaid's dress, zipped up in its garment bag. A spare tire, a case of soda, spare blankets. A stuffed animal?

The hail *hurt*. Globs of it landed in the trunk, as big as her fists. Where—was—the freaking—

There. A little white box with a red cross over the lid. Blair grabbed it, heaved the trunk closed, and ran back to the front seat.

Inside, David was doing a terrible job of applying pressure to his cut. His arm wobbled in the air. He looked close to passing out. Blair ripped open the first aid kit. "Logan, call 911," she barked.

"I don't have my phone! It went out the window!"

Blair pulled her own phone out of her pocket and tossed it back to him. Then she leaned toward David and pulled his arm toward her. Still a lot of blood. Technically, she should clean the wound first, but she didn't see any obvious dirt. More important to stop the bleeding. They could do a thorough cleaning later.

Blair slapped a gauze pad over the cut and pressed down hard. Behind her, Logan spoke into her phone.

"Hi, I—I guess we need an ambulance? We almost got hit by a tornado and all the glass in our car shattered, and my brother got cut . . . Hold on. Blair! Where are we?"

Blair glanced at the car's GPS and told him their exact location, which he repeated into the phone.

Hail bounced off the cracked windshield, pounded on the car's roof, came through the glass-less windows. A few chunks of ice landed in Blair's lap. She kept pressing down on David's cut, still trying to keep the arm elevated.

Ahead of them, off to the left, the tornado was thinning out. It narrowed to a ropey strand of air. Almost fragile-looking. More importantly: it kept moving away from them— heading northeast, toward the flat horizon. *Keep going*, Blair told it silently. *Don't come back this way.*

"We need to get out of here," David said. But his voice sounded confused, almost hollow.

Not like a guy who was holding in his real feelings. More like a guy whose feelings had short-circuited. *He's in shock*, Blair thought. *Maybe I'm in shock too. Do people in shock know they're in shock?*

Her brother reached weakly for the steering wheel with his good hand. "You can't drive like this, Dave," she said sternly. "And the car's not really drivable. But the tornado's gone. We'll wait for an ambulance to get here . . ."

Logan interrupted her. "I just lost the call! Blair, your phone's not getting any service."

Blair took a deep breath. *Stay calm. Do what David would normally do.* "The storm could be messing with cell phone towers. But they know where we are. They'll be here soon."

"Okay. Yeah." Logan suddenly sounded much younger. "You guys are soaked."

Blair glanced back at him. "So are you. I should've grabbed those extra blankets from the trunk. Sorry."

"I'm fine," said Logan. His voice wavered.

Blair tried to smile at him. "Good job with the call."

She checked David's cut. The bleeding seemed to have slowed. Gently, she moved David's hand over the gauze to the spot she'd been pressing. "Hold that right there," she said.

Back to the first aid kit. Roll of gauze: check. She wrapped it tightly—but not too tightly—around David's arm. Scissors: check. She cut the gauze strip. Adhesive tape: check. She secured the gauze in place. Done.

"Okay." Blair let out a long breath. "That should be fine till the paramedics get here. Just keep it up like that, to be safe."

"BLAIR!" Logan screamed. "There's another one!"

He was pointing out the back window.

Blair expected to spot another slender funnel dropping out of the sky. Instead, she saw a much thicker swirling mass. Like a fat, black V jutting up from the ground.

Up from the ground. It had already touched down.

The dust cloud at its base held countless dark specks, floating like confetti. It took Blair a second to realize those specks were pieces of wood and metal—objects the tornado had picked up in its path.

Blair's mind was racing.

They couldn't wait for the ambulance. They couldn't wait for anyone. They had to move—now.

3

"**D**ave, switch seats with me." Blair jumped out of the car and ran around to the driver's side. She barely felt the hail anymore.

When she opened the driver's door, David hadn't moved.

"David! Move over!" She unlatched his seatbelt and half-shoved, half-lifted him over the gearshift console and onto the passenger's seat. Then she slammed the driver's door behind her. "Logan, buckle up. This may not be a smooth ride."

Okay, you can do this. You know how to drive. Blair's driving instructor had always told her to take her time, to run carefully through her mental checklist and make sure she was "in tune with the vehicle" before she drove off. Rushing could lead to accidents.

Blair was pretty sure this advice didn't apply to her right now. As fast as she could, she scooted her seat up so that she could reach the pedals. With a sweaty hand, she adjusted the rearview mirror. The side mirrors were both badly cracked, so she didn't bother with them. *Guess today's not the day to practice merging onto the interstate.*

The parking brake was on. David must've done that by instinct. Blair took a deep breath, put the car in drive, and stepped on the gas. The tires crunched over a carpet of hail. With the hailstorm, the cracked windshield, and the mangled wipers, she could barely see. She leaned out the side window for a second, to check that she was in the right lane. Not that it mattered that much, since nobody else was driving on this road.

Her first time driving her brother's car. This wasn't how she'd pictured it.

"I think it's moving this way!" shouted Logan, who was watching through the back window. "Can you go faster?"

Do not try to outrun a tornado. You can't outrun a tornado.

What other choice did they have? Blair put more pressure on the gas pedal. The car was right on the verge of skidding. *Steady, steady . . .* "Logan, look for buildings—farmhouses, anywhere we might be able to take cover. Ditches, even. Like you said before—low ground. You see something, you yell. Okay?"

David had bought his car for its fuel efficiency, not for its off-roading capability. But she'd drive it through a wheat field if she had to.

The wind was getting stronger. Blair fought to keep the car steady. She had to sacrifice speed for control.

And they were almost out of gas.

Logan's voice edged up a notch. "It's gaining on us!"

We are so dead, thought Blair.

Just then, up ahead, another vehicle came into view.

The land was so flat that she could see the vehicle approaching from what seemed like miles away. As it got closer, she expected it to become recognizable as a minivan or a pickup truck or . . . anything that belonged on the road.

"What in the world . . ." Blair's voice trailed off. The vehicle was about the size of a van, but it looked like an alien spaceship. It had a streamlined body covered in what looked like metal plating. There was a hump on top that looked sort of like a tank's gun turret. Several weirdly-shaped antennae jutted out from the roof.

It zoomed past them before Blair could figure out what it was.

But one thing was clear: that vehicle was heading *toward* the tornado.

Blair slammed on the brakes and threw the car into reverse. Time for the fastest, sloppiest three-point turn in history.

"Blair, what are you doing?" demanded Logan.

"I'm following that thing."

"What?! Why?"

"Because it looks like it might actually survive a tornado."

Driving toward the funnel was nerve-racking for several reasons. One: the thing was *massive*. Blair felt as if she was heading into the mouth of a monster. Two: the wind got even stronger. Three: the hail was still coming down. And four: she was going way too fast. But she had no choice if she was going to catch up to that . . . *thing* on wheels.

Through the cracks in the windshield, she could tell she was gaining on the vehicle. The hail started to let up, but the wind didn't. Blair saw more tree branches whirl past. Big slabs of wood. Pieces of pipe. A car door crashed into the road right in front of them. Blair swerved around it. The wind tried to keep her from straightening out. Any second now she might slide right off the road.

She fought the wind. Gripped the steering wheel as if she was choking it. Managed to stay on the pavement.

Accelerating against the wind was almost impossible. Almost.

A few seconds later, she was right on the mystery vehicle's tail. Across the smooth, metal-plated back bumper, someone had spray-painted *THE BOSS* in bright red bubble letters.

Blair started honking.

"Do SOS!" said Logan. "Three short, three long, three short."

"Brilliant!" Blair said. She banged out three short blasts of the horn, three longer ones, then three shorter ones.

The other vehicle sped up.

"I don't think they're gonna stop," said Logan.

"They have to." *Because if they don't, I've just driven us straight into the path of a tornado. And used up the last of our gas.*

She veered into the left lane. Pulled forward, alongside the vehicle. Still honking. "Wave to the driver, Logan! Try to get the driver's attention!"

She sensed Logan flapping his arm frantically from the backseat. "Hey!" he shouted out his glass-less window. "HEY!"

Blair pulled ahead of the vehicle. It still wasn't responding to her horn.

She swerved into the right lane, angling the car sideways, like a police cruiser blocking an intersection. She knew she wasn't leaving the oncoming vehicle much time to brake. If the driver didn't react fast enough, it would slam right into the passenger side of David's car. *Please don't hit me, please don't hit me, please don't kill my brothers . . .*

The monster van screeched to a stop with inches to spare.

Blair engaged the parking brake—the car would need it in this wind. Then she unbuckled her seatbelt and leaped out of the car.

She'd thought she was prepared for the wind this time. She was wrong.

It was way stronger than it had been a few minutes ago. Blair remembered the torn-off car door she'd had to steer around. She dragged herself around the front of her brother's car. Her nose filled with the sharp smell of dirt.

The tornado was right there, looming over her—a black whirlwind blotting out the sky. She had no idea how far away it actually was. Hundreds of yards, maybe a mile?

A door of the mystery van opened— not the way a normal car door opened. It flipped up, like the lid of a trunk. Someone jumped out. A short, young-ish guy with dark hair and a goatee, maybe in his early thirties. Not happy.

"You idiot! What are you doing?"

"I'm sorry!" Blair said quickly. "But can we get in your vehicle?"

"What?"

Blair couldn't tell if he hadn't heard her or if he didn't get it. She raised her voice, shouting above the wind. "*Can we get in? Please! There's nowhere to take shelter! And our car's in bad shape. I don't think it can take another hit. Please!*"

The guy's expression flickered. Now he looked almost . . . amused. "You chased us down so you can hitch a ride with us?"

"I chased you down because your van looks like the sturdiest thing around." I *don't want a ride, you idiot. I want shelter.*

The wind ripped at Blair's clothes. She felt like she was getting blasted in the face by a hair dryer. David's car was starting to rock back and forth. *Enough of this*, Blair thought. Forget asking for permission. They were getting in this monster van.

Blair opened David's front passenger door. David looked like he was trying to follow the plot of a very confusing movie. She took her older brother by the arm and pulled him out of the car. "Logan, come on!" she called.

Logan jumped out, and Blair herded both of her brothers toward the monster van. Up close, it looked even weirder. Several thin, white tubes were strapped to the side, toward the back. Attached to each corner was a long pole with a spear-like point at the bottom.

The guy hadn't moved. "Please," Blair said again. "There's only three of us. If you can just fit us in for a few minutes, until—"

Something hit her between her shoulders. She had no idea what. A burst of pain shot through her back. But she gritted her teeth and kept moving toward the yawning door of the monster van.

The driver's window of the monster van rolled down. A young woman with curly purple hair stuck her head out. "Seriously, Sam? I *told* you their horn was beeping SOS. Get these people in here!"

"Right." The guy—Sam—flashed Blair a wry grin. He gestured toward his van's side door. "Welcome to our humble Tornado Intercept Vehicle."

Blair shoved her brothers in ahead of her. "Thank you," she said to the guy. But the wind was so loud now that he probably didn't hear.

"Come on, come on!" shouted the purple-haired driver. "Move it, Sam!"

Sam climbed into the car behind Blair, pulling the door down. And Blair found herself inside something called a Tornado Intercept Vehicle—seconds before a tornado hit it.

4

They were scrunched into the back of the van. Sam brushed past them to claim the only seat, which swiveled as he slid into it. There was just enough room for Blair and her brothers to crouch on the floor.

The vehicle's walls were covered with gadgets. Blair saw several screens of various sizes. Panels covered in buttons and dials. Cords and wires snaking everywhere. Next to the chair stood a contraption that looked like a beaten-up robot. Its metal body extended up into the bubble-shaped skylight overhead—the hump on the roof.

The wind was howling at a pitch Blair had never heard.

"I'm dropping it down!" called the purple-haired driver.

"Right here?" said Sam.

"I don't think we have time to get a better spot. If we don't drop now we're gonna get rolled."

"Okay, go ahead!"

Blair felt something shift along the sides of the vehicle. "What's going on?"

The driver glanced back at her. "Hydraulic panels. They can extend down to the ground. Blocks the wind. If wind can't get under the vehicle, we're less likely to flip over."

"Oh. Sounds good to me." *Be calm. Be cool. Be like David.*

Like David usually is.

"Show time," said Sam, grinning again. He grabbed the robot-device under the skylight. As he pressed his face against the gadget, Blair realized it was some sort of camera. "Here we go! Yeah, baby, come to papa! This is gonna be a good one, J.J.!"

"Should I launch a probe?"

"Yeah, launch it now! Right now!"

Blair couldn't see anything out the windows. Or at least, she couldn't make sense of what she saw. It was all just whirling darkness. But she could feel the wind blasting against the side of the vehicle. She could hear the bangs and pops of random objects hitting the armor.

Logan grabbed Blair's arm, and Blair pulled him against her. At the same time, she leaned into David. It finally sank in that they were all wet and shivering. Not shivering from cold. Not on a day as hot as this.

"We're in it!" shouted Sam, sounding like a kid on a rollercoaster. "Fantastic!" He swiveled in his chair, and the robot-camera-thing swiveled with him.

Blair's ears popped again. She didn't even remember them un-popping after the first time. The whole vehicle seemed to rattle, but it didn't lift off the ground. Those panel things must really work.

Then suddenly everything went still. Blair hadn't registered how loud the wind was until she heard it quiet down.

Logan opened his eyes, which made Blair realize she hadn't closed hers. It hadn't even occurred to her. She'd wanted to see what was happening.

"Yes!" whooped Sam. "That—was—awesome! We were right inside it! Good work, J.J.! That turned out to be a great position!"

"Don't thank me," said the driver. "Thank these random people. They're the reason we stopped here. If we'd kept going, we would've overshot."

"Oh, yeah," said Sam. For the first time he seemed to remember that he had guests. He flashed a smile that reminded Blair of Theo, her mom's new husband. People with that kind of smile weren't just in a good mood. They assumed *you* were in a good mood too. "Nice to meet you, folks. I'm Samir Chaudry—call me Sam. And that's J.J. Lyman in the pilot's seat. And our radar wizard is Silent Ron."

Blair hadn't even noticed the guy in the front passenger seat. He turned around long enough to give a quick nod. Silver hair, glasses, no smile. That was all Blair saw before he turned back around.

"Um," said Blair. "Hi. I'm Blair O'Neill. And these are my brothers, Logan and David—"

"What is *wrong* with you?" David cut in sharply. It felt like ages since he'd said anything. At first Blair thought he was talking to her, but then she realized he was glaring at Sam. "What kind of stupid stunt was that? We all could've been killed!"

"First of all, that 'stupid stunt' was part of our job," said Sam. His voice was calm, almost dismissive. "We're professional storm chasers. Not amateurs. We know what we're doing."

"No sane person would get that close to a tornado! Not even a storm chaser!" David was shouting now. Blair couldn't remember the last time he'd lost his temper like this.

"Most chasers wouldn't," Sam replied smugly. "But we're not most chasers. And secondly, you guys probably *would've* been killed if we hadn't come along. Care to see what shape your own vehicle is in now?"

He unlocked the side door and pushed it up.

Blair crawled over some wires and hopped out of the vehicle. David and Logan followed.

No more rain or hail now—just quiet air that smelled of wet dirt.

The tornado was moving away from them. Even as Blair watched, the funnel transformed—narrowing from a thick V-shape to a stringy, skinny coil. Slowly it started to curl up from the ground. As if someone had tossed a rope out of the sky and was now pulling it back up. The tail danced in the air as it retreated upward.

The road was littered with trash. Hay bales, wooden fence rails, roof shingles. Where had this tornado been before it reached them?

A power line lay in the grass, its wire snapped.

David's car was gone.

Blair swore. She thought of her purse, tucked under the front seat. The snacks in the glove compartment. Her bridesmaid's dress in the trunk. And then: *How are we going to get home?*

She fought the urge to cry. Instead she looked at David. "Dave, I'm so sorry. I didn't know what else to do."

Her brother shook his head, his expression numb again. "Not your fault, Blair. Not your fault. We're all here. That's what matters."

"*Ahem.*" Sam cleared his throat loudly.

Blair turned to him. "Thank you. Thank you so much."

"Our pleasure," said Sam. "Can we give you folks a lift somewhere?"

"No need," said David coldly. "We called for an ambulance a little while ago. We'll just call again."

Blair had forgotten about his arm. She looked at the bandage. To her relief, no blood was seeping through it. Then she thought about her own cuts and bruises— from the shattered glass, the giant hail, the debris that had hit her. She and Logan should probably get some first aid too, just to be on the safe side.

"Gonna take a while for emergency responders to get out here," Sam pointed out.

"Closest town is Aura. And this area's crawling with supercells. Another vortex could form any minute."

"Seriously?" said Blair. "After we already had two tornadoes that close together?"

Sam laughed. "You're not from around here, are you, sweetheart?"

Blair gritted her teeth. "One: don't call me sweetheart, or anything else in that category. Two: yes, you can give us a lift."

"Blair—" David started.

"Dave, we can't just stand here in the middle of the road for the next half hour. It's not safe. And at least their ride has, like, metal plating."

Sam's eyes flashed with pride. "Ten thousand pounds of steel armor. Bulletproof windows. All-wheel drive. Best place to be in bad weather, aside from underground."

David closed his eyes briefly, then looked at Sam. "Fine. You can drop us off in Aura."

"We're not going to Aura," said Sam cheerfully. "We're heading where the action is. Where to next, Ron?"

Inside the vehicle, a booming male voice said, "Hatchville."

5

Hatchville.

Where Blair's mom lived.

"I thought the storm system was moving *east*," said Blair. Her voice came out sounding angry. Which was probably better than sounding terrified. She suspected Sam didn't have much patience for fear.

"It *is* moving east," confirmed Sam. "But all the good stuff is still happening to the west of us. Couple of EF-3s already today. Might get an EF-4 or even an EF-5 if we're lucky."

"Lucky?" David burst out. "Are you out of your mind? The damage an EF-5 can do is—"

"Unbelievable," Sam finished for him. "We know. That's why we want to get footage of it. Plus, see these things here?" Sam pointed to the white tubes attached to the back of the vehicle. "These are wireless probes. We launch these into the path of a tornado. Then they transmit data back to us. Data for *science*. Experts use that to learn more about how tornadoes work. Could save lives one day. Anyway, point is, Ron says things are looking juicy near Hatchville. So we're going to Hatchville. And we don't have any time to waste."

Blair could tell that her brother wasn't done arguing. But Sam was at least partly right. They really couldn't afford to waste time. David wasn't going to bleed to death in the hour it would take to reach Hatchville. But if they stayed out here in the open . . .

"Well, how convenient," she said, working hard to keep her voice neutral. "Our mom lives in Hatchville. We just came from there. You can take us back. Thanks." Blair got back into the vehicle first. Logan followed her. David hesitated another minute, then gave in.

"Hit it, J.J.!" Sam called as he closed the side door.

The vehicle sprang forward. It moved fast, for something so bulky. The O'Neills sat on the floor again, scrunched among equipment on all sides. Sam settled into his chair and studied a screen mounted to the back of the driver's seat. "You can stay on this road the whole way to Hatchville, J.J. Unless we see anything we wanna chase."

Sam reached for a duffel bag that was zip-tied to the front seat. He pulled out three fluffy towels and tossed them to Blair. "Dry off, my friends. And here's the first aid kit. Use some antiseptic wipes for those cuts. Your face is pretty scratched up, missy."

"Blair," she corrected him, taking the kit he gave her. Bigger and fancier than the O'Neills' first aid kit. Which was now lost, along with everything else in her brother's car.

"Right, knew it was something short. You thirsty? Hungry? Nothing but the best for any passenger of the Boss."

"That's what you call this thing?" said Logan, rubbing a towel over his wet hair.

"Oh yeah." Sam spread his arms as if he could wrap the whole vehicle in a hug. "Once, this was an ordinary SUV. Now it's a state-of-the-art Tornado Intercept Vehicle. Chasing storms since 2013, baby."

David made a disgusted noise in his throat. Blair shot him a questioning look. She would've understood if he'd been shaken up, but she hadn't expected him to be so—hostile.

She decided to do what she always did when David was upset: change the subject. "So this is what you do for a living?" Blair asked Sam as she toweled off.

"Yep. We're making a documentary. Got the funding through some online kick-starting. Our goal is to get as close as we can to tornadoes—while staying safe. And we've gotten some amazing footage lately. This spring and summer have been our best season yet."

Blair swiped an antiseptic pad over the cuts on her arm. She used a fresh pad to dab at her face. The cloth came away red. For the first time, she felt the sting of the cuts. "And those probe things?" she asked.

"Oh yeah. That's the scientific part of the job. We launch those up, and they take all kinds of readings from inside the vortex."

"The vortex?"

"You know." Sam made a spinning motion with his finger. "Wind funnel filled with dirt and debris, with a hollow core? Ring any bells?"

Blair gritted her teeth at his tone. She gently felt the biggest cut on her face, deciding if it needed a Band-Aid. Her back ached a little in the spot where some unknown flying object had hit her. She expected to find a bruise the next time she checked in a mirror.

"Anyway, the probes measure wind speed, pressure, things like that," Sam went on. "It's all about figuring out what's happening in there. There's still a ton that we don't know about tornadoes. About how they form and why they act the way they do. Why most of them move northeast but some will randomly change direction. Or why some grow to be two miles wide and stay on the ground for almost an hour, when most don't do that. The more we know, the easier it is to predict a tornado. Warning people sooner means fewer casualties. Wins all around."

"And I'm sure you make plenty of money selling the footage you get," said David dryly.

"You bet." Sam didn't seem to notice David's attitude. Or he chose not to care. He flashed his shameless smile again. "Plus, we're making a profit from the web series now."

"That's more of a win for you than for humanity," David pointed out.

"Sure, but who's keeping score?"

David's nostrils flared. "Let me check your bandage," Blair said quickly. It still looked secure. Hardly any seepage. Blair wished she could see what was going on inside her brother's head just as easily. But she had no idea why he was being so confrontational with Sam. She'd hardly ever seen David this worked up.

"But my dream," Sam continued, "is to get inside the eye."

Blair knew he was waiting for one of them to ask *What's the eye?* He was having too much fun showcasing his mission. Meanwhile her family was still bloody. So she just said, "Mm-hm?"

"*The eye of the tornado.*" Sam's voice was hushed but intense. "Dead center. Hardly anyone's been inside it and lived to tell about it. Maybe two, three people in the past hundred years. You get footage from inside the eye of the tornado, and you become *legend.*"

"Yeah, I'll bet it'll go viral on the Internet for a whole fifteen seconds," muttered David.

"Whatever. See what you think when my documentary wins, like, ten Oscars. Hey, Ron. How long before the action hits Hatchville?"

"Probably forty-five minutes. Hour at most."

The fear surged back into Blair's stomach. That was her mom's town they were talking about. Her mom's house . . . "Mind if I make a call?"

"Not if you keep it quick. We've got a lot going on in here. Ron's monitoring radar, I have to navigate, and we need to listen to the local weather reports. Gotta keep the background noise to a minimum."

Blair turned to Logan. "Hey, can I have my phone back?"

Logan fished it out of his jeans pocket and handed it over. Blair noticed that his hand shook a little. She scanned him for untended cuts, but he'd cleaned up well. "You okay?" she asked.

He nodded. She smiled as if she believed him. Then she glanced at her phone. Stroke of luck: it had service again.

Her mom picked up on the second ring. Blair updated her as quickly as possible—which wasn't easy, because her mom kept interrupting with little shrieks. "Oh, Blair! The car's completely *gone*? I can't believe this! That could've been you! You could've—"

"Yeah, but we're fine," said Blair firmly.

"Even David? You said he got cut."

"He's doing okay. He'll need stitches. But I'm keeping an eye on the bandage in case he starts bleeding again." She expected David to react when she mentioned him. But he was just staring blankly at the robot-camera. His anger and aggression had disappeared as suddenly as they'd bubbled to the surface. What was going on with him? Had he hit his head somehow? Was this a concussion? What were the signs of a concussion . . . ?

Focus, Blair scolded herself. *Talk to Mom.* "I'm worried about you and Theo, though," she went on. "Sounds like you might get some tornadoes of your own. Within forty-five minutes."

"We're expecting that. Happens all the time. It's unusual for them to be forming this early in the day, though. If I'd known you were going to get caught in this—"

"You couldn't have known," Blair cut her off. "It's not your fault, Mom." She couldn't help glancing at David. In his opinion, almost everything was their mom's fault somehow.

"Where are you now?" her mom asked.

"We're heading back your way," Blair told her.

"What? How?"

Blair glanced at Sam, who was giving J.J. directions. "We're with the tornado chasers."

She heard her mother suck in her breath. "I don't think that's a good idea."

Blair sighed. "Neither does Dave. Neither do I, actually." Still no reaction from David. Either he was deeply fascinated by that robot-camera, or he was totally checked out.

"Can't you have them drop you off at the closest town?" said Blair's mom. "I can come get you—"

"That's an even worse idea," Blair said. "You shouldn't be going anywhere with the weather this bad. And the only towns between here and Hatchville have a population of, like, ten. They don't have their own emergency responders. They don't have hotels. What would we do? Knock on some stranger's door and ask if we can share their storm shelter?"

"But these storm chasers—they're taking risks. They could put you in danger. If I just—"

"Mom. Stay where you are. *Don't leave your house.* That would put *you* in danger. We'll be okay. We're only an hour east of Hatchville. We'll be there before you know it."

Her mother was still protesting when Blair said "Gotta go now, love you," and hung up.

"An EF-4 touched down just south of the state line," said Ron. He had an amazingly deep voice. The kind of voice that could do dramatic voiceovers for movie trailers: *IN A WORLD . . .*

Sam whistled in appreciation. "I bet Gehrig's team got a slice of that. But I've got a good feeling about Hatchville."

Blair suddenly felt sick to her stomach. This guy was excited that a tornado might hit her mom's hometown. He actually envied other teams of storm chasers that might be closer to the action. Blair found herself echoing David's earlier question: What *was* wrong with this guy?

Logan had a different question. "What are those numbers you keep saying? Like EF-4 and whatever?"

"That's how we rate tornadoes," said J.J. from the front. "The Fujita scale, invented by a brilliant scientist named Ted Fujita.

It measures how destructive a tornado is. EF-0 is the least destructive, and it goes up to EF-5."

"So what was that tornado we ran into back there?" Logan asked.

"That was a little guy—an EF-2 at the most. Wind speeds of about 115 miles per hour, I'd guess."

If that was an EF-2, the one we ran into earlier must've been a baby, Blair thought. *A very destructive baby.*

"Still fun, though," added Sam. "We were in an awesome position. I bet we got some great footage."

"Yeah," snapped David, out of nowhere. "Great footage of something that trashed other people's lives. Well done."

Sam held up his hands in a sarcastic surrender gesture. "Whoa, chill, man. We're not happy that tornadoes cause damage or that people get hurt. But storms like this happen whether we watch them or not. Might as well get the most we can out of them."

David opened his mouth to respond. But at that moment, Ron's voice boomed through the vehicle.

"Guys, we got another one."

6

Blair half-stood, trying to see out the windows. "Where? Where is it?"

She felt as if her stomach was inside a washing machine, getting churned around. A fast, confusing, painful spinning. But also weirdly . . . exciting.

"We're not in range yet," said Ron. "Big wall cloud about fifteen miles north, guys."

"Okay, let's do it," said Sam. "I'll find you a road, J.J. Sit down, sweethea—" He paused when he saw the look Blair gave him. "*Ahem.* Blair. Make yourself comfortable."

"We *are* comfortable," David told him—not convincingly. "But we'd rather be safe. Can't you just head straight to Hatchville?"

Blair could tell that Sam was only half-listening. "Aw, where's the fun in that?" he said.

"We're not having *fun*!" David exploded. "Nothing about this is fun for us! We're shaken up—cut up. We've lost our car. And now our mom's town could be in danger—"

"Look, I get it." For the first time, Sam sounded truly annoyed—offended, even. "But my mission is to study and film tornadoes. And I've got a news flash for you. Everything that's happened to you today? It's happened to a lot of other people in this area. You're not special. And you'll be putting yourself in a lot more danger if you leave this vehicle now. So just sit tight. We'll get you to Hatchville."

David clenched his teeth but didn't say anything else.

Sam hunkered down over his roadmap screen. "J.J., there should be a dirt track coming up in about five hundred yards. Turn right and stay on that . . ."

Blair watched as the three team members worked. Ron explained what he was seeing on his radar screen. Sam navigated. J.J. turned off the highway onto a path that felt much bumpier. And above them, the clouds hovered. Blair kept glancing up through the window in the roof. It was like watching the troublesome kids when she lifeguarded. She had no doubt that a disaster was looming. She just didn't know when it would happen or how it would play out.

"Here we go," said Ron.

Sam had a better view from his chair than the O'Neills had from the floor. He looked out the side window and whistled. "Check out these beauties. Hold it right here, J.J., I wanna get some wide shots."

He flipped up the side door. Warm wind rushed in, strong but not overwhelming. Sam grabbed a handheld camera from somewhere and hopped out.

Blair followed him.

She barely heard David say, "Blair, stay in the van—"

She was already outside, staring at the view.

They were on a narrow dirt road now, far

from the highway. Blair could see a cluster of buildings in the distance. A white-gray farmhouse, a red barn, a tall grain silo. The house looked about the size of her thumbnail, so she guessed it was at least half a mile away. And maybe two football fields to the right of the buildings, she saw—what, exactly? She wasn't sure.

Mini-tornadoes. Or ghost tornadoes. Four or five slender white funnels. Rising out of the ground but not quite connecting with the swollen, churning cloud above them. Each narrow funnel seemed to bend and sway in its own rhythm. One funnel faded away completely, like mist, in half a second. Then another materialized out of thin air.

Sam was filming with his little camera. "Aw, man, look at those vortices!"

"I didn't know there could be more than one vortex," Blair murmured.

"Oh yeah. Amazing, isn't it?"

Blair wasn't comfortable admitting it, but— yeah. It *was* kind of amazing.

It was like a dance—the graceful swaying of these wispy, thin funnels. From this distance, she couldn't hear anything unusual. No threatening roar, no rain or hail striking objects on the ground, no glass shattering. Just a steady, regular wind. The weaving motions of the vortices looked almost peaceful. They seemed to be taking their time. Performing.

And this could just *happen*. Several times a day, even. Like it was no big deal.

One of the mini-twisters veered to the left, toward the farm. It seemed to sweep gently over the barn. Blair almost didn't realize what had happened.

Then she saw the debris.

The building just flew apart. Walls, roof, everything lifted into the air and orbited around the vortex, looking feather-light.

"Ohmygod," Blair gasped, all in one breath. "That barn—"

"Yeah, that looks rough," said Sam. "Good thing it was just the barn. Hope nobody was inside."

"Blair, *get back in here!*" shouted David.

But Blair couldn't move. Her eyes were glued to those delicate, deadly spirals on the horizon. She watched as the vortices drifted closer together. They made her think of strands of hair on the verge of weaving together in a braid.

"Oh man," breathed Sam. "Moment of truth."

Suddenly one vortex seemed to grow wider, more solid. A couple of the other vortices wisped up into the spiraling cloud overhead. The rest seemed to feed into the main vortex. All the energy from the cloud now went straight into this single, full-sized funnel. One giant white vortex.

At least it looked giant to Blair. Maybe it was only another EF-2.

Ron leaned out his window. "Sam, looks like it's moving northeast, like normal."

"Right." Sam clapped a hand on Blair's shoulder. Personal boundaries clearly weren't this guy's strong point. "Better get moving again," he said. "Let's see how close we can get."

Blair shrugged his hand away. "Aren't you worried about that farm?"

"I don't control the weather." He jumped back into the Boss. "I just follow it."

Blair followed him back into the vehicle, not bothering to point out that this wasn't actually an answer.

Five seconds later, J.J. was driving toward the new tornado.

"You've got to be kidding," said David. "You need to get *closer*? This is insane."

"Aw yeah." Sam was back in his chair. His eyes darted between the side window and the roadmap on his screen. "This one's a beast. Hang a left up here, J.J. We'll come at it from the side."

"Careful," said Ron. "It's moving fast."

Blair scooted toward the side window. If she rose up on her knees and craned her neck, she could see out. The funnel was moving away from the farm. J.J. was gaining on it. The van bounced along, in and out of mud-filled ruts.

Ron again: "It's turning, J.J. It's turning around!"

"Okay," said Sam. "You can make a right turn in a few hundred feet. That'll get us out of its path—"

J.J. hit the brakes. "Tree trunk. Right across the road. I gotta back up." She put the Boss in reverse. "Where's the closest side road behind us, Sam?"

"Uh, about three hundred yards back . . ."

Now Blair saw it. The turning. The gentle arc of movement as the twister switched directions.

Sam drew a harsh breath through clenched teeth. "Holy—we're in a really bad spot. Make it fast, J.J."

"I'm going as fast as I—"

The Boss stopped moving.

7

"**G**et us out of here, J.J.!" Sam shouted.

"I'm trying! We're in a rut! These freaking farm roads . . ."

"You're going to get us killed!" David yelled.

"*Shut up, David!*"

The words burst out of Blair before she knew what she was saying. David just stared at her. She stared back, as stunned as he was. "You're not helping," she added in a feeble voice.

David's whole body seemed to shrink slightly.

When was the last time Blair had shouted at her older brother? The last time they'd had a fight, a *real* fight? She doubted either of them could remember.

J.J. rolled the Boss forward, then backed up again with more momentum. The van dipped as it went into the ditch again, then rose and kept moving. Blair looked out the window again.

The tornado cruised toward them. Blair watched as it glided straight through the farmhouse.

More debris free-floating in the air. Blair felt sick to her stomach.

"Here, right here! Here's the side road!" Sam called to J.J.

J.J. made a hard left turn and zoomed forward again. She made so many more turns in the next minute that Blair lost track.

"It's shifting again," said Ron. "Hold up, J.J. Let's see what it does next."

Blair didn't breathe. She just waited, with everyone else in the van.

Slowly, she registered that the tornado was changing directions again. It was moving away from them.

"Okay, let's move in again," said Sam.

Blair couldn't imagine doing this all the time. Get close, retreat. Get close again. Hold your breath and hope you're making the right call. Wait to find out if you die.

J.J. retraced the Boss's route, looping around the path with the fallen tree. The storm was rolling away fast now.

Blair's eyes locked on the farmhouse.

Or at least, what was left of the farmhouse. It was now a pile of rubble. Wooden frames and pieces of siding looked like splintered toothpicks. Blair saw scarred patches of ground where other buildings— the barn, the silo—had been ripped away. The surrounding land—wheat stalks and all—had been flattened.

"We stopping, Sam?" asked J.J.

Sam hesitated. "We'll lose the storm . . ."

"Are you kidding me?" Blair burst out. "We have to stop! What if someone's trapped in there?"

"I know, I know, take it easy." Sam let out a weary sigh. "Pull in, J.J. See what's up."

J.J. turned onto the narrow, rutted dirt track that led to the house. Blair felt the Boss's tires grinding over debris, but J.J. didn't slow down. *She's used to this*, Blair thought. *Not just the chase and the storm itself. The aftermath. They're all used to it. They must see disasters like this all the time.*

The Boss rolled to a stop in front of the wreckage. Sam released the locks on the side door and pushed it up. Everyone jumped out. Logan brought the first aid kit. Blair noticed that no one had to tell him to.

Up close, the ruined house looked even worse. Blair could see actual objects—bits and pieces of ordinary household items. To her left: part of a chair. To her right: half a picture frame. Straight in front of her: a toaster oven. Ten minutes ago these things had all been whole. Now they were garbage. Blair remembered the time in elementary school when Logan ripped up her art project. He'd had a tantrum because she was too busy to play with him. In the blink of an eye he'd ruined hours of work. She'd been furious . . .

Sam cupped his hands around his mouth and hollered, "Hello? Anybody here?"

Silence.

A heavy sludge seemed to settle in Blair's gut. How could anyone survive this?

"Maybe no one was home," said Logan in a small voice.

"We'll find out for sure," said Sam grimly. "Spread out. And be careful—no fancy stunts. Watch out for glass, nails, sharp stuff. If we find somebody who's trapped, we'll call 911. If we find a body, we'll try to pull it out."

Sam's carefree attitude was completely gone. He might as well have flipped a switch.

"You stay here, Logan," said David. "Hold on to that first aid kit in case we need it."

Logan nodded. He didn't push to be included in the search. Blair half-expected David to ask her to hang back with Logan. But he just gave her a look that seemed resigned and proud at the same time. Blair thought of how she'd shouted at him a minute ago. She'd spent so many years being David's backup, his "copilot." But today she was the one calling the shots, and for the first time, he seemed willing to accept that.

At first they all just circled the outer edge of the house. Blair kept her eyes peeled for a hand, a foot, a flash of hair. Just like lifeguarding, when she had to scan the water for bobbing heads and flailing arms.

Then J.J. waded into the mess, stepping over splintered wood and chunks of insulation. Sam followed her lead. They picked their way toward the center of the house. Blair watched them for a minute—watched how they chose each step carefully. Watched the way their eyes moved. Watched how cautiously J.J. shifted a mangled coffee table to check what was under it. This was an art.

Off in the distance, maybe fifty yards away, Blair saw a twisted heap of metal. A car. Red, smashed.

The sludge in her stomach rose up to her throat. "Guys? Should someone go check out that—that car?"

She pointed. Her finger was shaking. Was the rest of her shaking?

Ron nodded. Wordlessly, he headed toward the crushed vehicle.

Blair looked away. If that car belonged to the people who lived here . . . Well, maybe they had two cars. Maybe they drove off safely in their other car. Maybe they were on vacation in Mexico. Or in Antarctica—the one continent that never got tornadoes. The Internet had taught her that ages ago, when her mom moved here and Blair was worried.

Blair's eyes roamed over the remains of the house. There was actually some sun peeking through the clouds now. How weird. The feeble light glinted off random objects buried in the mess. A cracked mirror. An antenna. The porcelain corner of a bathtub . . .

The bathtub.

The place her mom's neighbors hid when there was a tornado warning. The safest place to be if you can't get underground.

Blair plunged into the debris, keeping her eyes fastened on the visible bit of the tub. She wove her way over and through a grim obstacle course. A small voice in the corner of her mind seemed to know what to do.

Don't trip over that bent floor lamp.

Be careful scrambling over that pile of wood. It could collapse under you.

Watch out for that broken window pane.

Almost there. The tub was mostly covered by fragments of the roof. Blair couldn't see much. "Hello?" she called, even though Sam had tried that already. "Is there anybody—"

A moan.

Coming from inside the tub.

Blair charged forward. There was a tiny gap between the tub's rim and the slab of roofing that sat on top. Through that gap, Blair saw a patch of dark hair.

"Someone's here!" she screamed. "Guys! Help me! Someone's in here!"

8

Blair couldn't have moved the roofing on her own. Luckily, Sam and J.J. moved fast. Even David managed to pitch in with his good arm. About ten seconds later, Sam was helping a middle-aged man sit up in the bathtub.

He had a deep gash on his forehead and another on his shoulder. His whole body was covered with grit. But he was conscious, and he could move.

"Logan!" Blair shouted. "The first aid kit!"

Her younger brother was already making his way toward them.

"Logan, be careful!" warned David.

Meanwhile Sam was talking to the guy.

"Can you tell me your name?"

"Uh, Walter Letzmann."

"Was anyone else in the house with you?"

"No. My wife's visiting her sister . . ."

In Antarctica, I hope, thought Blair.

The man looked around slowly. Blinking in the sunlight. Seeing the damage to his house for the first time. Realizing that he no longer *had* a house—that his whole life had been blown apart in a few seconds. Blair couldn't imagine what he was thinking.

Or maybe she could.

***

"Ambulance is on the way." Sam hung up his phone. "Coming from Hatchville Memorial Hospital. Should be here in twenty minutes."

"Good," said David. "Then if the paramedics don't mind, we'll ride along with Mr. Letzmann."

"Oh, I see how it is," said Sam. He gave them that bullet-proof playful grin again. "You're ditching the Boss."

"My brother could use some medical attention too," Blair pointed out. "Plus, if we stay with you any longer, I think you'll give him a heart attack."

Sam laughed. "Fair enough. Maybe we'll run into you in Hatchville."

"I hope not," said David. "I hope nothing hits Hatchville."

Sam nodded. "Sure. I'm just saying, the Boss is a freaking fortress. There's no place I'd rather be when a tornado's coming my way."

David just shook his head. He didn't look angry anymore—just exhausted.

Blair said quietly, "I believe that. But we're at risk no matter what. I think we'd rather face those risks with our family. No offense."

"None taken. Good luck with that, swee— *Blair*." He smiled. She almost smiled back.

***

Twenty minutes later, paramedics lifted Walter Letzmann onto a gurney. Everyone else hovered around, watching—awkwardly silent, until J.J. spoke to Blair.

"That was good thinking," she said. "Smart to look for the bathtub."

Blair shrugged. "Glad we found him." She paused. "I'm glad you found us too. Really. I don't know what we would've done if you hadn't come along."

J.J. smiled. "Technically, *you* found *us*."

Another pause. The paramedics settled Walter inside the ambulance.

"Most days aren't like this, you know," J.J. said quietly. "Most days are boring. You drive around, look at the radar, listen to weather reports. Storms fade without doing much. Or you don't reach them in time for the magic. So you drive some more. You make a lot of guesses. You guess wrong most of the time. So when you do see a tornado, it's like: finally, payoff. Most people don't do this just for thrills. If they want reliable excitement, they can—I dunno—go bungee jumping. To really do this, you have to be patient. And careful."

Blair raised her eyebrows.

"Yeah, I'm serious. You have to calculate all your risks. Nobody actually wants to get killed on a chase. You have to weigh every single choice. And you have to really, really love the storms themselves—just seeing what nature can do. That has to mean more than all the days when nothing happens. And all the days when the worst happens."

Blair nodded. She had to admit that she at least partly understood.

Her brothers were squeezing into the back of the ambulance now. Blair climbed in with them and looked back.

J.J., Sam, and Ron were already heading toward the Boss. Ready for the next chase. Just before the paramedics closed the ambulance doors, Sam turned back. He flashed his cocky grin and saluted her.

Then the doors shut, and the O'Neills were headed for Hatchville.

9

David didn't say a word all the way to Hatchville Memorial Hospital. When Blair asked if he was okay, he just nodded.

Weirdly, Logan talked to Walter. Talked about his favorite bands, the food at their mom's wedding reception, the fact that he couldn't text some girl he liked because his phone had been blown away by a tornado earlier this morning.

Normal stuff.

Walter seemed to be listening carefully.

Meanwhile, Blair texted both her parents to explain what was happening. Their dad was probably in a meeting with his phone off, but her mom called her back immediately.

"I'll pick you up," her mom said firmly. "No arguments. The hospital's only ten minutes away from our house. I'll bring you home as soon as David's gotten his stitches. Can I talk to the boys?"

Blair handed the phone to Logan. When her younger brother finished chattering at their mom and passed the phone back, she looked at David. "Mom wants to talk to you too."

"I'm good."

"David . . ." But Blair didn't know how to finish that sentence. She settled on "Mom loves us." It seemed better than *Snap out of it* or *You're worrying me*.

David sighed. "I know." Well, that was something, at least. "I'll talk to her when we get there."

Great, thought Blair. *Awkward family reunion, Round Two. Now with a hundred percent more tornadoes.* As if they weren't all stressed enough. If only they'd left Hatchville an hour earlier this morning. Then they would've missed the severe weather, and David would be done brooding. And none of them would have to deal with the *Is-Mom-really-back-in-our-lives?* question again until winter break.

Then Blair looked at Walter Letzmann. A man who didn't know for sure if his wife was okay. A man who was going through the scariest experience of his life, surrounded by a bunch of strangers.

Strangers who were explaining the difference between black doom and sludge metal.

Blair took a deep breath. "Hey, Mom. Dave's napping right now. We'll see you soon, though. We all love you."

***

Blair spent the next hour tracking the weather on her phone. At the hospital while David got stitches. On the ride from the hospital to their mom's house. And in the living room of that house, while everyone else talked.

Their dad had called, and their mom put him on speakerphone while Logan gave everyone a play-by-play of the morning's events. ". . . And then Blair just straight-up *dived* into the other lane and cut them off. Like, I've never seen a turn that fast. Except in movies. It was so freaking cool. And then they let us all get in their tornado-mobile . . ."

Their dad's voice crackled through the phone. "Blair, honey, I'm so proud of you. You've been incredibly brave." At the same time, their mom walked over to give Blair a hug.

"I mean, I couldn't have done it all by myself," Blair pointed out. It felt odd to be treated like the hero of the whole strange experience. Especially when she had the feeling that this ordeal wasn't over yet.

After the call with their dad ended, the living room got quieter. Rain drummed on the roof. Blair could hear the wind wrapping around the house, searching for a way in.

Staring at radar images on her phone was making Blair feel woozy. She wished her mom or Theo would turn on the TV or the radio. But both of them were just getting on with their day. Theo was in the kitchen baking. Blair's mom sat on the couch writing wedding thank-you notes. Just a typical Sunday for them, tree-bending winds included.

"Shouldn't we be in the storm shelter?" Blair asked her mom.

Her mom shrugged. "We'll head there if something actually touches down near us, but it'll be pretty cramped with five of us. No point scrunching in there unless we have to."

This happens all the time here, Blair reminded herself. She forced herself to put her phone down. Theo was telling David about the time he almost cut his whole finger off and needed a million stitches. Blair noticed that David was listening politely, not looking too broody. She chewed on a piece of banana bread that Theo had made. The tension in her shoulders started to fade.

And then the siren sounded.

That long, high-pitched wail meant only one thing. "Okay, everybody," said Theo calmly. "Time to get in the shelter. Follow me out to the backyard."

Nobody panicked. Nobody ran. They all moved quietly to the back door.

The panic set in when they stepped outside.

"It's right on top of us!" yelled Theo.

Thanks, Theo, thought Blair in some non-terrified corner of her mind. *Really helpful.*

The tornado was crashing through houses three blocks away. Fragments of houses spurted into the air.

Nobody needed to be told to run.

They ran in an awkward clump. Theo clung to Blair's mom, who had one arm around her new husband and held Logan's hand with the other. Blair held on to Logan, with David bringing up the rear. Blair was sandwiched between brothers, trying not to trip them.

The wind no longer sounded like wind. It was just a deep, earth-shaking roar. Not like a train or a jet engine—not like anything Blair had ever heard.

Blair's mom pulled open the hatch to the storm shelter. She pushed Theo in ahead of her and then pulled Logan after her.

Blair was on the top step of the shelter when a wooden beam flew toward them. The tornado had blown it from another yard, another house. Blair ducked as it hurtled through the air.

It hit David instead of her.

She whipped around just in time to see him sprawl backward. He landed hard on the wet ground, pinned under the slab of wood.

"Dave!" Blair screamed. She felt like she was running in slow motion. Partly because the wind was pulling at her so powerfully. She had to fight for every step. When she reached David, he was already trying to sit up.

She didn't think about whether the wooden beam was heavy. She just shoved it off him. Then she grabbed him under the arms and hauled him up. Together they staggered back to the storm shelter's entrance. The door stood upright, wavering from the impact of the wind.

David would've stopped her if he'd been strong enough, if he hadn't been dazed and injured. He would've made sure she got into the shelter first. She knew that. He'd spent her whole life protecting her. He was the one who'd taught her how to be brave in the first place.

She pushed her brother through the entrance. And when the door blew shut behind him, she let it close. She knew she couldn't fight that wind. But she gripped the handle with both hands, hoping to anchor herself.

The next thing she knew, she was airborne.

10

The wind lifted Blair as if she weighed nothing, tearing her hands away from the door handle. She couldn't see, couldn't breathe.

Cover your head . . . But she couldn't control her arms. Her whole body flailed wildly, gripped by different strands of the wind. She was hurtling through space, too fast for her brain to keep up.

I'm going to die, she realized. J.J. had said she was smart. Her dad had called her brave. She'd held on to that door with every ounce of strength she had. And she'd still gotten sucked into this tornado. She was still going to die.

Because this wasn't about being smart or brave or strong. It was about being lucky or unlucky.

Suddenly she was plummeting. The next thing she knew, her whole left side slammed into something incredibly hard. The ground.

She screamed from the pain. Curled up into a ball. Realized that she could control her limbs again, that the wind wasn't fighting her.

The wind, in fact, was gone.

Everything was dead still. Blair looked up. Above her, she saw the tornado. Lifting silently off the ground as if it weighed nothing. As if it wasn't carrying houses and cars in its air currents. It was just winding itself back up into the sky. Directly overhead, Blair could see straight up into the tornado—straight into the eye that Sam had talked about.

She saw sleek spinning walls of wind. Flickers of lightning darting out from the walls. Little baby funnels, twisting horizontally, delicate as pieces of string.

Blair couldn't breathe. But she stared up into the eye of the tornado until the clouds closed over it.

She sat up—slowly, because it hurt. The tornado was gone. The air was motionless. Somewhere far away, she heard her family calling her name.

"Blair! Oh my g—Blair!"

That was when it hit her. *I'm alive. Awesome.*

***

Blair ached all over. Her left wrist felt as if someone was hitting it repeatedly with a hammer. Probably broken—sprained at the very least. But she could walk. She could see. She wasn't bleeding. Well, not seriously.

Absolutely everyone had hugged her. Her mom was sobbing with relief. Even Logan was crying. David gripped her by the shoulders and said she was out of her mind, and amazing, and *out of her freaking mind.*

Blair couldn't help noticing the damage, though. Her mom's house was pretty much fine, but all through the neighborhood, buildings were flattened. The tornado had chewed them up and spit them out. Piles and piles of wreckage stretched in a crooked line all the way to the edge of town.

And already, people were searching for survivors. Citizens of Hatchville waded through the rubble. Some called out names. Others just yelled, "Does anyone need help?" Nobody was just sitting around waiting for ambulances to show up.

Blair stood up slowly. No dizziness: good. And her feet held her weight. She should probably get checked out for a concussion, just to be safe. Not to mention sprained or broken bones. But there was plenty of time for that. According to her phone—still in her pocket, still working—it wasn't even noon yet. She still had the whole day ahead of her.

***

It was a long day. Hours of going from house to house, helping to pull people out. Not everyone had made it. Blair suspected she would cry at some point. But by the time she had a chance to just sit and think and feel, she was exhausted. Too exhausted to think or feel. Which just left sitting.

Incredibly, she herself wasn't badly hurt. Just a sprained wrist and the promise of a monstrous bruise on the whole left side of her body. David was basically all right too. The impact of the wooden beam had mashed up his right shoulder. So by now, his right arm could audition for a zombie movie. But all the important pieces were intact.

David sat down next to her in their mom's kitchen. Everyone else was in the living room.

"I wonder if Sam and J.J. and Ron got to see this one," said Blair.

"Probably," said David dryly. "They seemed to be on a roll today." He paused. "I know you think I was rude to them."

"No. I think we were all scared and upset. And they were kind of insane. I understand why you didn't, like, bond with them."

David closed his eyes and tilted his head toward the ceiling. "That Sam guy. This is going to sound weird, but he reminded me of Mom."

"Um . . . okay. I admit I didn't see a resemblance."

"You know the way Mom jumps into new things. The way she gets excited about what's next—about what it means for her. And how she never thinks about the consequences."

"I—don't actually know if that's true, Dave," Blair said quietly. "That's how it seemed to us, after she left. But—we didn't know what was going on in her head. And I don't think she ever forgot we existed. I think she's always cared."

David propped his elbows on the table and rested his head in his hands. "Maybe you're right. I don't know."

"You could try talking to her about it. We could all try having more honest talks, once in a while."

"That's fair," he sighed. "But my point is, that's why I was so tense with the chasers. It was like, these people take risks for fun, when everyone else needs help just staying alive. And at the same time, I felt . . ." He swallowed, dropped his arms, and straightened up. "I mean, there we were, depending on them.

Because *I* messed up. *I* couldn't get us out of that situation."

"Dave—"

"After Mom left us, I had one goal. To always be there for my family. To keep you safe and never let you down."

Blair swallowed. "You've never let us down, Dave."

"But today—"

"No, not even today. You're not letting anyone down." She squeezed his good arm. "You can't protect us from everything. That's not your job. Not as a brother, not as a replacement parent. That's not something *anybody* could do."

He let out a laugh that was at least fifty percent sob. "I guess you don't need me taking care of you, anyway. You took charge when I lost my grip. You're the reason we survived."

"Yeah," said Logan, entering the kitchen. "We totally don't need you around anymore, Dave. I'm calling the factory and sending you back."

This time David's laugh was steadier.

Logan grabbed a piece of banana bread. "Hey, I found Sam's storm chaser web series. I'm watching it online right now. It's *epic*."

He left again. Blair snorted, "Guess he's not traumatized."

David shook his head. "Seriously, though, I couldn't stand those guys. Storms like this—they're not a game. They don't exist to give people excitement. They destroy people's lives."

"I think most chasers get that. I think most of them really want to help save lives. They're not just in it for the thrill. Even Sam's crew."

He nodded slowly. "What about you?"

She stared at him. "What about me?"

"I can tell it's interesting to you. The way tornadoes work. The idea of staying one step ahead of them."

Blair popped a piece of banana bread into her mouth and chewed for a minute. "I don't know. Part of me did enjoy it, maybe. But a bigger part of me was just glad to make it out alive—glad that we're all okay. I've never been that scared in my life. I'd be fine with never being that scared again."

David put his arm around her shoulder. She leaned into him, feeling all the bruises and scars on her body. Finally, for just a moment, she closed her eyes.

The image of the tornado's core danced behind her eyelids. Still terrifying and beautiful—half nightmare, half miracle.

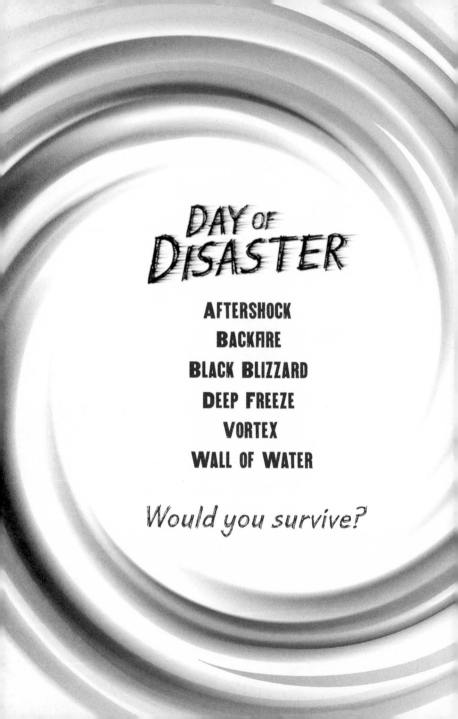

DAY OF DISASTER

AFTERSHOCK

BACKFIRE

BLACK BLIZZARD

DEEP FREEZE

VORTEX

WALL OF WATER

Would you survive?

About the Author

Vanessa Acton is a writer and editor based in Minneapolis, Minnesota. She enjoys stalking dead people (also known as historical research), drinking too much tea, and taking long walks during her home state's annual three-week thaw.